The Dreidel That Wouldn't Spin

A Toyshop Tale
of Hanukkah

By Martha Seif Simpson

Illustrated by Durga Yael Bernhard

❖Wisdom Tales❖

Library of Congress Cataloging-in-Publication Data Simpson, Martha Seif, 1954- The dreidel that wouldn't spin: a toyshop tale of Hanukkah/by Martha Seif Simpson; illustrated by Durga Yael Bernhard. pages cm. Summary: The most beautiful dreidel a shopkeeper has ever seen will not spin for the two children who insist they must own it, but perhaps it would spin for a child with the true spirit of Hanukkah in his heart. ISBN 978-1-937786-28-1 (hardcover : alk. paper) [1. Dreidel (Game)--Fiction. 2. Behavior--Fiction. 3. Hanukkah--Fiction. 4. Miracles--Fiction. 5. Toy stores--Fiction. 6. Jews--Fiction.] I. Bernhard, Durga, illustrator. II. Title. PZ7.S6073Dre 2014 [E]--dc23 2014016126.
Production Date: June 2014, Plant & Location: Printed by 1010 Printing International Ltd, Job/Batch #: TT14050861
For information address Wisdom Tales, P.O. Box 2682, Bloomington, Indiana 47402-2682, www.wisdomtalespress.com

To my relatives with roots
in the Old Country
M.S.S.

To Gwendolyn Tapper
D.Y.B.

It was the most beautiful dreidel the shopkeeper had ever seen. The Hebrew letters *Nun, Gimmel, Hay,* and *Shin* glistened against the brightly painted colors on its four sides. "*Nes gadol hayah sham,* 'A great miracle happened there,'" said the shopkeeper to himself.

The peddler held it up. "Notice how it is hand-painted on the finest wood. This is one of a kind."

"I'll take it," the shopkeeper said.

"Hanukkah begins in two days, and I have already sold all my dreidels. This one should fetch a handsome price."

"Perhaps," said the peddler, "but the miracle of Hanukkah cannot be bought."

"That may be," the shopkeeper said. "But right now I am more concerned with turning a profit than I am in miracles." He placed the dreidel in the display window.

That afternoon, a man and his daughter strolled
into the shop. They carried packages from the
most expensive stores in the town. The shopkeeper
admired their finely tailored garments.

"Choose anything you like," the man said.

The girl raced through the shop, piling toys up on the counter. The shopkeeper rubbed his hands in anticipation as he mentally added up the sale. When the girl finished, her father paid for the items and started for the door.

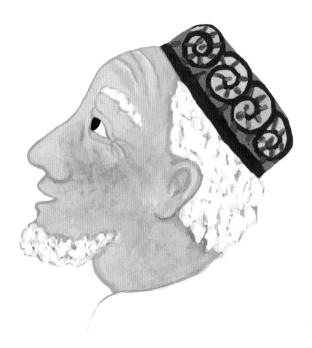

"Wait!" shouted the girl. "I need a dreidel."

The man surveyed the store. "There are none here. We will look elsewhere."

"Excuse me, sir," the shopkeeper said. "This should please your daughter." He carefully lifted the dreidel out of the window and placed it on the counter.

The father read the price on the tag. "So expensive!"

The girl stamped her foot. "But I want it!"
The man shrugged. He paid the shopkeeper
and left with his daughter.

The next morning, they rushed into the shop.

"Thief!" cried the man. "This dreidel doesn't work!"

"What do you mean?" the shopkeeper asked. "How can a dreidel not work?"

"Look!" the girl demanded. She stood the dreidel on the counter and gave it a twist. But instead of spinning, it just fell over.

"You see?" she asked.

The shopkeeper sighed. "Well, then, what would you like in exchange?"

"Scoundrel!" hissed the man. "I spent a tidy sum here yesterday. I demand my money back, or you will face the consequences!"

The shopkeeper turned pale. Such an important man could ruin his business. "Of course, sir. Here you are. I don't wish to argue."

The man took the money and stormed out the door with his daughter.

"How can a dreidel not work?" the shopkeeper wondered. He stood it up and gave it a twist. The dreidel spun smoothly for a minute, then slowed down and came to a stop.

"There's nothing wrong with it," mumbled the shopkeeper. Even so, he was shaken enough to reduce the price before replacing it in the window.

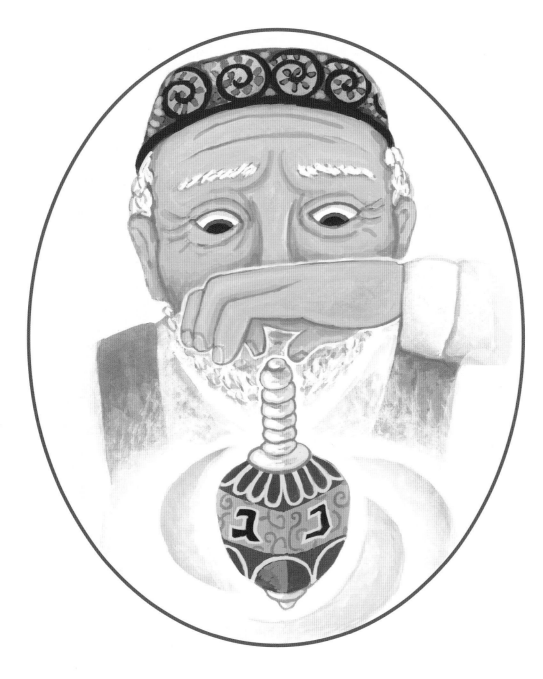

Soon afterward, a woman and her son arrived. They dumped their bulky packages onto the floor. The shopkeeper observed how well fed they looked.

"We want to see that dreidel in the window," the woman demanded.

"Certainly," the shopkeeper answered. He gingerly picked it up.

The boy grabbed it from his hands. "This is much bigger than my other dreidels. Buy it for me, Mother."

The shopkeeper forced a smile as the boy repeatedly tossed the dreidel into the air and caught it. "Surely you wouldn't deny your son a new dreidel for Hanukkah?" he asked the woman, keeping a watchful eye on his merchandise.

The mother pulled out her purse. "Children today, they want everything!" The shopkeeper gave a quiet sigh after they left.

The next morning, the couple burst through the door. "Cheat!" accused the woman. "You sold us a broken dreidel!"

The shopkeeper watched as the boy tried to spin it and failed. Not wishing a repeat of the previous day's outburst, he quickly refunded the money. After they left, the dreidel again spun without trouble for him.

"I don't understand it." He shook his head and removed the price tag. Regretfully, he slipped the dreidel onto a shelf behind the counter.

That afternoon, a man and a boy were gazing into the shop window. They carried no packages. The shopkeeper noted the patches on their ill-fitting clothes.

Shyly, they opened the door. "Pardon us," said the man. "We have no money to spend. But it is almost Hanukkah, and your toy shop is so cheerful. May we come in, just to look?"

The shopkeeper hesitated. But no one else was in the store, and the boy looked so hopeful. He gestured for them to come in.

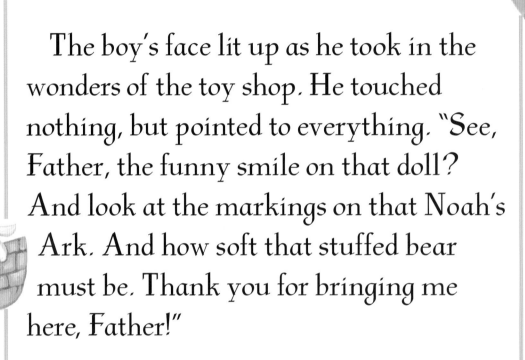

The boy's face lit up as he took in the wonders of the toy shop. He touched nothing, but pointed to everything. "See, Father, the funny smile on that doll? And look at the markings on that Noah's Ark. And how soft that stuffed bear must be. Thank you for bringing me here, Father!"

The shopkeeper's heart was touched. Here was a child who saw beyond price or appearance, one who understood what was truly precious.

The man put his arm around his son, and then turned to the shopkeeper. "Thank you, kind sir, for allowing us into your wonderful store. May you be blessed by the miracle of Hanukkah."

"Wait, friends," the shopkeeper called as his visitors turned to leave. "I would like you to have this." He gently held out the dreidel.

"It's beautiful!" the boy cried. He gazed at the bright, joyful colors and the letters that sparkled like a *menorah's* candles. "It looks just the way Hanukkah feels, doesn't it, Father?"

"This dreidel is indeed special," agreed the man. "We cannot accept such a fine gift."

"Yes," said the shopkeeper. "The dreidel is beautiful. But twice I have sold it, and both times it was brought back because it wouldn't spin. You would be doing me a favor by taking it."

After thanking the shopkeeper, the boy turned to his father. "May I try it?" he asked. The father nodded.

Gently, the boy stood the dreidel onto its tip. Then, with a quick flick of his fingers, he gave the stem a twist.

The dreidel spun gracefully on the counter top, its letters shimmering amidst the swirl of colors. They watched in awe as the dreidel spun for several minutes, longer than any dreidel they had ever seen. At last, it stopped and fell onto one side.

They all blinked in astonishment. The letter *Gimmel* had transformed into the letter *Koof*, and another letter, *Shin*, had changed to the letter *Pay*!

The shopkeeper immediately understood why. "<u>N</u>es <u>k</u>atan <u>h</u>ayah <u>p</u>oh," he said quietly in Hebrew. "A <u>small</u> miracle happened <u>here</u>!"

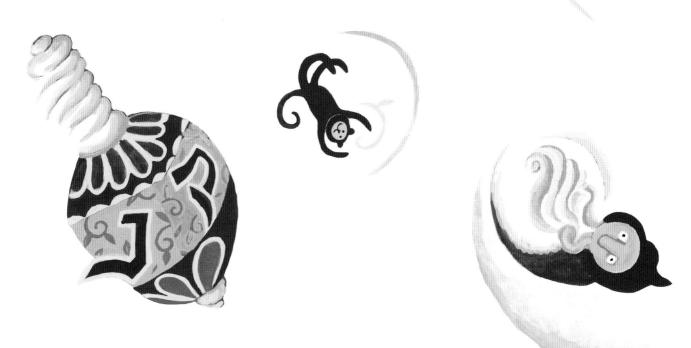

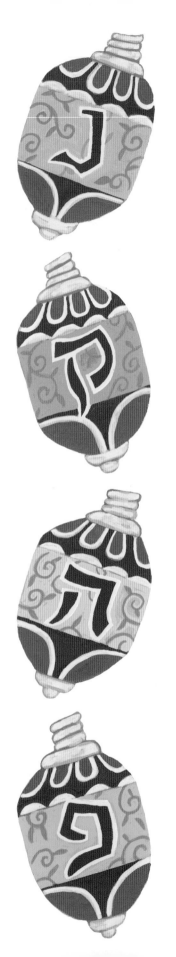

"This dreidel was clearly meant for you," the shopkeeper said after a pause. "Please take it. And may it bring you much happiness."

As he watched them
walk away with their
treasure, the shopkeeper
recalled the peddler's words.
Though many people came
to his toyshop, it had taken
a boy of simple means
to remind him that the
miracle of Hanukkah
truly could not be bought.

Author's Note

Hanukkah

Hanukkah is a Jewish holiday that is known as the "Festival of Lights" or the "Feast of Dedication." The holiday occurs around the time of the olive harvest in Israel, which is usually close to the time of Christmas. Hanukkah lasts for eight nights and celebrates a miracle that occurred long ago.

The miracle happened like this: The ancient Jewish Temple in Jerusalem had been captured by cruel invaders sent by Antiochus, the Greek emperor, in 165 BCE (Before Common Era). Following many battles, the invaders were conquered by the Maccabees, a group of brave Jewish warriors. After the Temple was reclaimed, it needed to be rededicated. However, there was only enough olive oil to keep the *menorah* (a sacred lamp) lit in the Temple for one day. But miraculously, this little bit of oil lasted for eight days and nights, which was enough time to press and prepare more oil. It is this miracle that Jewish people still celebrate today by lighting a candle in their homes and synagogues for the eight nights of Hanukkah. Special blessings are recited as the candles are lit at sundown each night.

Many Hanukkah customs are popular in the Jewish tradition, including serving foods made with oil such as potato pancakes (*latkes*), giving gifts of chocolate coins known as *gelt*, and playing a game using a dreidel.

Dreidels

A dreidel is a top decorated on four sides with Hebrew letters. The table below shows each letter and what it stands for on a dreidel. In the story of Hanukkah, the letters signify the phrase *Nes gadol hayah sham*, which means "A great miracle happened there." This refers to the miracle of the oil lasting for eight days; "there" refers to Jerusalem. The sounds of those four letters are also used to represent instructions (in Yiddish) on how to play a dreidel game.

Hebrew Letter	Name of Letter	Stands for	Meaning in the Dreidel Game
נ	Nun	nes (a miracle)	Take nothing
ג	Gimmel	gadol (great)	Take everything
ה	Hay	hayah (happened)	Take half
ש	Shin	sham (there)	Put one item into the pot
ק	Koof	katan (small)	*Our story also uses these two Hebrew letters*
פ	Pay	poh (here)	

Appendix: How to Play the Dreidel Game

This is how the dreidel game is played. First, players decide on what items to use as tokens. This can be any small item, such as chocolate coins, marbles, or pennies. Next, they divide the tokens evenly among the players. At the beginning of each round, everyone puts one token in a center pile which is called "the pot." The players then take turns spinning the dreidel. A player must take or put in a token according to what letter faces up when the dreidel stops spinning:

Nun – The player takes nothing from the pot
Gimmel – The player takes everything in the pot
Hay – The player takes half of the pot
Shin – The player puts one item into the pot

If a player has no more tokens, he or she is out of the game. The player who collects all the tokens is the winner.

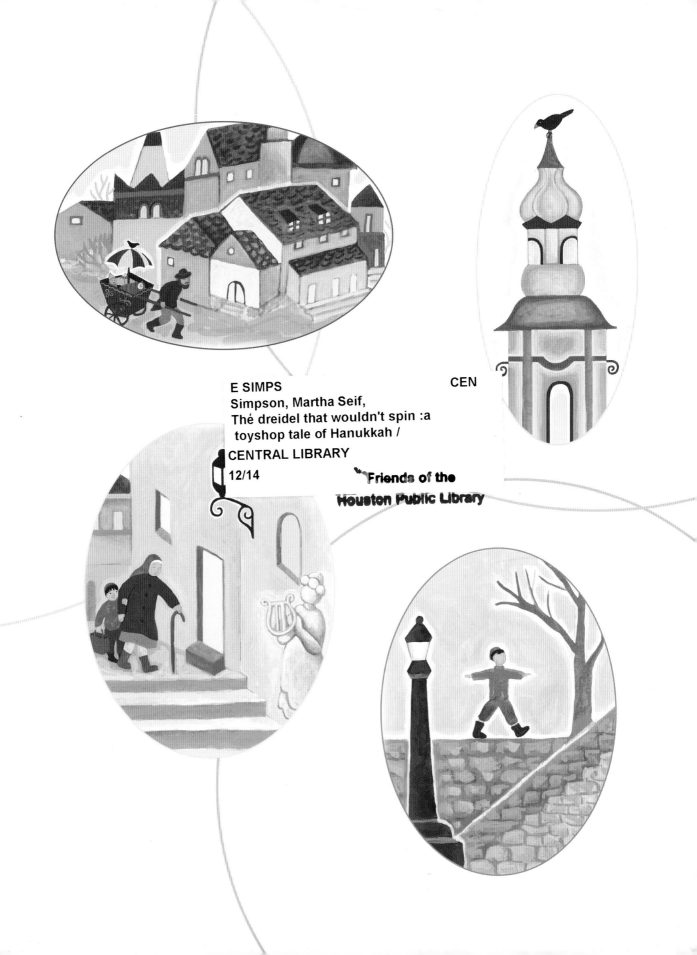

Friends of the
Houston Public Library